ONE THING

A novelette

XANTHI BARKER

ᴓPEN PEN

First Published in 2019
by Open Pen, 25 Crescent Road, London, E13 0LU

openpen.co.uk

978-1-9164136-2-7

OPNOV003

OPEN PEN NOVELETTES #2
"One Thing"
First Edition
© Xanthi Barker & Open Pen
Edited by Sanya Semakula
Cover illustration by Pierre Buttin - pierrebuttin.com
© Pierre Buttin

For B.M.

0

There's no word for what Len is.

That's what he realises, sitting in the motorway service station cafeteria, listening to the couple further along the table listing all the relatives they may or may not invite to some party or holiday they're planning, trying to figure out how in one morning he can have lost Violet, his van and a contract he was a week away from finishing. There's a pain in his chest when he thinks about going home, as though going home is the problem. As though if he stays here long enough it won't be true that Violet is dead.

If she'd been his wife, he'd be a widower. But if your ex-wife dies, you're left with nothing at all.

He needs to ring his daughter. Her mother is dead and he hasn't rung her. He tried to ring her when he first heard the news but the line was busy and then he was late for work. He should've gone home right then. Should've told them what happened and driven straight home. New Forest to London, he could've done it in just over an hour if he'd left at seven. Now it's half past two and whether it's the traffic or the weather or something in Len, getting back is like dragging himself through tar. He rearranges his feet under the table, takes the lid off his coffee and sips it. No they don't make words for what he is.

A little girl with the face and stature of a piglet sitting at the next table shouts, "Give it back!" Her screech pierces the room and Len jerks around, watching the faces of people nearby flash irritation, before catching the eye of her attractive velour-suited mother. The woman turns away from him, swatting the boy beside the girl and giving her phone to the girl. The girl pulls the screen to her nose, her knuckles going white with grip. Len shakes his head in admiration. The list of things he wants back could go on forever. He counts six before he's had a second sip of coffee.

1. His van. The Green Goddess. A 2001 VW Transporter in racing green (resprayed twice in its lifetime, once just last year), a cassette player and the kind of hard, thin steering wheel that no manufacturers produce anymore, manual windows with rough black handles, a good hard smell of diesel and a good hard rattling as he drove. That feeling of the parts of the engine clicking into step with each other, scratch under

the driver's door keyhole, dent to the left grill, captain seats and a photo of his daughter stuck in the back, so's not to distract him.

2. The last three months of his life.

3. Knuckles. Good, working, trustworthy knuckles. No bumps, no scars, no painful callouses. Knuckles that could punch and not floor him.

4. That grey corduroy shirt with the button-down pocket. Hard to get a shirt that fits these days. Hard to get one that doesn't make him look like a creep. Hard not to look like a creep anyway since he's lost weight, gained those pervert rings around the eyes.

5. His daughter as a baby. Actually, it would do to have her as a baby for just one day. That day being a damp one, twenty years ago, mid-November, not a day he'd want back at all but for one tiny thing at the end of it. The day Violet left. She said she was leaving and then she left. She walked out and shut the door and he walked back along the hall and climbed inside the airing cupboard, shut that door like it was only a game of shut doors they were playing, pulled the bristling orange padding out of the coat the boiler wore and stuffed it in his mouth and screamed. Stayed there a long time. Longer than he should've done. Too long. It was getting

dark when he climbed out. The room was reflected in the window. His arms and legs moved without him. He didn't know where he was going at first, until the sounds made shapes he recognised.

Lila was crying. That was what it was. Sense coming back to him. Bad man. Stayed away too long. Selfish man. Didn't want to come back. Her cries like fish hooks in him. He went to her. Fibreglass cuts stinging inside and out of him. He watched his hands pick her up. Little wet rocking thing. The shiver of her. How long had he left her? Doesn't want to remember. That little wet shivering thing. Remember this: lifting her up. She was breathing. And he was grateful to be breathing then so he could see her breathing, breathe with her and learn her breath, and he held her there, the two of them breathing. And she reached up and slapped him across the face. She did. Her little fat milky fist, sticky and swollen beneath that fragile baby skin that could just burst and leak the whole blip of her life to a dirty stain on the already-dirty carpet and then nothing, in an instant. She smiled at him. That smile — as much of Violet as he should have needed — that, there — he wants that back.

6. Ah, fuck. It's too much now. Forget it.

That's the problem with death. It flirts with you.

It makes you want things it's not favourable to want. None of these things has happened outside Len's imagination in a long time. He's had other girlfriends. He's even once almost had a wife. A new wife. A second wife. *My second wife.* How extravagant it sounds. He has friends, a daughter, a profitable (if precarious) talent, a driving license, two arms, two legs, strong heart, strong lungs, thoughts in his head, things to do. Most importantly, he has perspective.

That shirt he lost one night in a hostel somewhere between Birmingham and Norwich. His knuckles he left in chunks and blood in various towns across the country. That van. Don't think about the van. The three months, well, you're never too old for another fucking learning experience. It wasn't his most prestigious job either, the loss of it wouldn't ruin him. A three month contract restoring three separate roofs on a country farmhouse and lodge a few miles outside a town called Pilley that itself had barely fifty inhabitants: it should've been straightforward. It was. Ninety-five days of dawn to dusk labour behind him, meticulous with his research to match the original styles and materials — one type of corner slate he drove to Devon to source — six days left to go and his daughter, his friends, his flat, even

5

his neighbours, the self-declared Mad Ali in the flat above and passive-aggressive Barry and his speech-less mother below, even them he'd been keeping in his imagination of the future like the three shepherds kept that Jesus star. And then, just when he was about to be released, to have the pleasure of an invoice to write and the final payments to come in, he dropped the ball. Forgot the ladder, mismatched the grout, dropped a box of tiles Mrs Sable was intending for the bathroom smashing all 240, cut an extra 2 inches off the cherry wood beams because he was thinking the number 20 instead of the correct 22 inches, reversed into an ancient yew, totalled the Green Goddess and the tree, incurring a £2500 fee from the local tree surgeon and botching his insurance claim by telling more of the truth than even the billionaire owners of the yew, the manor and the land advised him to do.

Ah life.

All for nothing: three months of his life, plus at least another month preparing, another getting the job, not to mention weeks of pitching for others and the work he'd turned down because of it and the equipment, the materials, the research — six months at least, gone. He might as well have been in prison, except then he would've had visitors, rehabilitation services. Len's landed himself with a big fat sheer nothing. Had to borrow the family's butler's Audi to get his tools home and himself off the ruined property, hanging his head so as not to see Eric's dismay at all that grease and metal pressing on the cream leather. Eric will pick it up on Monday, and presumably they won't talk, though they had a beer together on four separate occasions over the past few months and even once went to the cinema.

The whole thing will come off Len's pay, a joke because there's nothing left of it anyway. He counted sixteen times the woman at the bank said, What? when he tried to explain what happened.

So how can he ring Lila? He should've driven back to be with her straight away, told Mrs Sable he was taking a few days off. He didn't give himself time to think. Things happened too fast. It's a fact that shame can eat at the insides of a man as severely and suddenly as caustic soda.

He'll call Lila when he gets home. He has to call her.

Not yet.

Lila called him while Mrs Sable was inspecting the tree and he couldn't answer. He saw his daughter's name and slipped the phone back in his pocket, watched the scars on Mrs Sable's reconstructed nose glinting in the sunlight. You've broken my heart, she said. As if she couldn't have it surgically replaced. With Len's mistakes, there was no way the house would be ready in time for Mr Sable's sixtieth birthday party. A tragedy, she said. *You can imagine how a wife feels, Lennard?*

So she'd seen his wedding ring, then.

It was absolutely typical Len Ward.

But he didn't say, No I'm afraid I can't Mrs Sable, my wife left me before we reached our fourth anniversary, never once wished me happy birthday after that, nor our daughter, and in fact she died last night and the man she left me for rang to tell me this morning, do you know how that feels? Ah yes — such is life.

"Such is life," she kept saying. "These things happen. Only you don't expect to pay for them."

She was referring to the first two payments she'd already made. But there was work Len had done which was salvageable, weeks of it. He wasn't losing out on that. Besides, he'd already spent it. Amazing how quickly money can sink into a life that's been starved of it. Of course, she'll be contacting her lawyers. Of course, Len doesn't have protection like that.

She asked Eric to "sort this out" and excused herself

for a homeopathy appointment. Len packed his things in silence while Eric watched from the doorway. His phone kept ringing so he switched it off.

Ah, life. He drinks cold dregs of coffee and crosses his boots under the table. It'll be two hours from here, at a good run. He can't check the traffic without his phone. He hasn't figured out the car's radio yet. It's stuck on a channel with a radio drama about a man plotting to murder his wife.

Len drinks the nothing that's left in his cup and spins it on its base. It falls over and brown drops of liquid spatter across the table. He snorts. It's always like that, isn't it? Nothing left that you can use but enough to ruin someone else's day. Or in this instance, sleeve and book.

He looks up at the woman who's been sitting opposite him all this time, hunched over a book. She must be mid-sixties, scraggly hair under a neatly tied shawl and big rimless glasses. She sits up, staring at her sleeve, at the coffee sinking into the pages. Len sets the cup upright then crushes his face into his palm. "God, I'm sorry," he says.

He stands up, looking around for something to wipe it up. But she waves her hand, smiling at him. "I was thinking exactly the same thing," she says. She sighs, shuts the book and slides it into her bag. "I don't know what I'm supposed to have done, but it's helpful to think he's punishing me, that it hasn't all been for nothing."

Len stares at her. He blinks and stares and she continues to smile at him. He realises he should say something, hears her words again in his head. "Is it that bad?" he says.

She laughs. "It's that bad. And you?"

Len raises his eyebrows. Her expression doesn't change. He cuffs his head. "It's that bad. I'm thinking of changing my name."

"What name would you choose?"

Len shrugs. "Always thought if I had a son I'd call him Jacob."

"Jacob what?"

"Well my name is—"

"Not your name. They'll track you down, remember?"

"Okay. Jacob — Ladder?"

"Like the song?" She starts to sing it, loud enough to make Len much too aware of their neighbours.

"Oh," he says. "That must've been why it sounded good." He steps behind his chair, looks around for the exit.

"Are you off?" the woman says.

"Got to go."

"Start your new life."

"No, home."

She holds out her hand and he stares at it for a long time before she reaches over and grabs his, shaking it. "I'm Nelly," she says. "See you then."

"My wife died last night."

"I see."

"And not only that but I lost my job. And not only that but I totalled my van. And not only that but because of certain mistakes I made, I won't be paid for half the work I've already done. I'm bankrupt. I don't know if I'll work again."

Nelly stares at him for a long time and it feels as though she is looking at every mean, broken part of him. He thinks he shouldn't have told her all that and how he always says too much when someone gives him the time. But then she leans back in her chair, frowning up at him. She looks like she is working something out. Then she says, "My wife died too. Six years ago. I miss her."

"Your wife?" Len says. He sits down again.

"She wasn't really my wife, I suppose. She died before they changed the law."

"My wife wasn't really my wife either."

Nelly narrows her eyes and then nods. "What's a word anyway? I used to call her my *life*. That's how I'd introduce her: 'Oh this is Linda, my wife, sorry, I mean my *life*'. It got a laugh more often than you'd think."

"Well," Len says, "I mean. My wife divorced me."

"Divorced and died? You're like Henry the Eighth."

"No. Twenty years ago she divorced me. Then she married someone else. Then she died."

"Ah."

"Yeah."

"You cheated on her?"

"No!"

"She did."

"Well."

"Oh."

"Money?"

"You could say."

"Took the children? Poisoned them against you? Told them Ted Balls was their real father?"

"Ted Balls, that's about it. No. Well. I think sometimes that would've been better, more bearable. I could've told myself she wanted the best for our daughter. A life for her. God knows I was no catch — more broke then than I am now, if that's possible. She didn't take to mothering so I did the childcare, left my job, she still wasn't happy, moved out — no, met a man and moved out — no, started up with a man she already knew and moved out and — err — honestly, she ran off with her accountant, Ivan of Ivan P. Stokes & Co. LLC. Ivan who she found in the *Yellow Pages*. Who could've guessed? Didn't see either of us again."

"Never again?"

"For four years, anyway."

"Like an Olympian."

"Not like an Olympian. She let the torch go out."

"You resent her. She abandoned you both."

Her eyes meet Len's and he smiles. "I love her. I'm madly in love with her. Like a teenager. I've never loved anyone else. I'll admit it to you, what difference does it make? I'm pathetic. I'm a spineless cuckold. I hate her, of course I hate her, but honestly, I don't know anymore if there's any difference."

"You still wear her ring."

Len notices he's fiddling with it. "My knuckles," he says.

It's true that his callouses are too big to remove it. But it's also true that he had many chances before the bone began to jut, not to mention the number of people he

13

knows who could cut it off in two minutes if he asked them.

"It's a long time to wear a ring."

"I love her."

"She's dead now."

"If you tell people your ex-wife died, they imagine you must be happy."

"Are you?"

He gives her a look. Nelly stands up. Her jeans are fixed by a plaited leather belt. She hoists her bag onto her shoulder and pulls her jacket tight around her. "Thirty years together and my life's family wouldn't acknowledge me," she says. "They were very religious. She used to say for them religion came before everything, even God. They wouldn't allow me at the funeral. They said —" she laughs — "'She doesn't belong to you.' Well, I thought, one good thing from all this, now she doesn't belong to them either. In death we belong to no one — isn't that wonderful, Jacob Ladder? Take your wife on holiday, buy her an ice cream, give her a new name. Go to bed with her. Get drunk on champagne and vodka. It could be your honeymoon. She could be your new life."

"Can't drink," he says. "Had to give it up."

"Get drunk on the good memories, then."

"She liked ice cream. Banana splits and Cornettos."

"Likes," Nelly says. "People don't change."

"Do you want an ice cream?"

"I really do have to go."

"Oh," he says. "OK."

She smiles, her mouth twisted in on itself, and then gathers her things and walks off. Her hair at the back is silvering and her shawl, he realises now, was the reason he found her so familiar. It was red cotton, patterned with flowers, the type worn by the brash old ladies who used to rule Kilburn High Road in the eighties when he first ran into Violet. *Ran into*.

He was running. He was late. He rang the bell, rain in the back of his shirt, fag unfinished. The bell made his finger fizz, the old mechanical style. He'd ask her that day, would not be able to stop himself — after all she'd been nice, brought him tea and toast, made a joke about roofless/ruthless that he couldn't remember after, goddammit — if she'd mind if he opened it up to have a look. It was slightly off-kilter. He had the tools, he wouldn't break it. It was an antique. He just had to ask. And she had this smile like that was exactly the thing she'd always wanted and wanted from exactly him. She could smile like that back then. Lila's smile.

They took it apart and laid the pieces on a threadbare

but pristine white tea towel on the hall carpet like one of those designer's exploded drawings. They were on their knees staring at the parts, going, "Oh my God" and "Can you believe the size of it?" and "That tiny hammer!" Their voices getting mixed up like they were already completely inside each other, as wound tight and interconnected as the springs and cogs and soft brass.

He reassembled the bell and fixed the roof and she told him to come back later that evening and she'd get some beers in for them. When he came back he rang the bell and she opened the door like that itself was the mechanism, his wanting her turning through cogs and sounds, the swinging wooden door, until there she was, looking right at him. That same night he kissed her. Two years and he married her. They were born on the same day, same year, two hundred miles apart, what kind of coincidence? Her in a rented bedroom on a backstreet in Ladbroke Grove, her mother an unmarried dancer. Len in the waiting room at Birmingham General, his dad fainting on the floor beside them.

Len didn't know, had never imagined the sun would come out in his life like that. He had settled on overcast drizzle for the most part, women who thought he couldn't think because he didn't think to say every thought he had, didn't make the regular kind of jokes, hadn't begotten a career path or benefactor (parental or otherwise) by the hoary age of 33, hadn't realised 501s were out of fashion last decade and you were supposed to be clean-shaven and have acrobatic choreographed sex punctuated with orgasms even the first night and six beers in, well. And what do you think other men made of him? Too slow with his quips and precise with his hands, reading novels on his breaks and afraid of beer, mad for one woman only.

She was the first person in his life that made him want to say things, the first woman in his life to say the word children to him, let alone suggest, let alone insist on one. She said she couldn't live without him. She couldn't sleep without him in her bed — *his* body, *this* body, coat-hanger thin, a coating of hair not thick enough to be sexy but still widespread enough to make visitors to it itch or frown if he wore short sleeves, arms too long, hips too low, arse-less, with "those big craggy ribs" as his aunts had enjoyed pointing out when they first erupted in him — *that* body — it was that body Violet could not sleep without. She slept on his left side, her head on his arm, her breath across his chest, her left leg hooked over his. He used to lie on his back and stare at the ceiling and wonder about it. She talked in her sleep, a language he didn't know, something ancient, ancestral, her grandmother's Polish. He recorded her on cassette and they listened back and she said it must have been leftover from some other life. But there was no other life. This was it.

Life. Wife.

What happened after that still didn't make sense — had someone spiked their life, dragged it off to some filthy warehouse, murdered it on some concrete floor? It didn't make sense. He had everything. And then it was gone.

Violet divorced him and married her accountant, a man she once described as *criminally boring*. It was written in law books, civic forms, certificates. Ivan and Violet Stokes. Violet Stokes & Co. LLC. She married him. And now she's gone. Same as Nelly in her eighties shawl, solid council houses, chips in newspaper, the *Yellow Pages*. Same as the Green Goddess, Jack Sable's birthday party, Len's career, talent, fortune, wife, life — life, life, life — years of it, all gone.

Really, there's only one thing he wants back.

6. Violet. He wants Violet. Not as she was, but as she had been. Violet before any of this. Violet who

chain-smoked and wore blue jeans and his old shirts. Violet who danced to their badly-tuned radio early Saturday mornings. Violet who cussed herself every time she looked in the mirror and drank straight gin with half a lime in it. And they watched *Have I Got News For You?* and *Blind Date* together every week and when she was pregnant he brought her litre cartons of tomato juice and she drank them with a straw. Like Len, she lost her mother young, and they both agreed they wanted to be as much in their child's life as possible. Where did that woman go?

Lila arrived. She grew teeth, started babbling, learned to walk, outgrew her baby clothes, and then Violet fit everything she owned into two suitcases and left.

My wife died.

My life died.

Len grits his teeth and thumbs his eyes, crushing the paper cup in his hand with a loud sound that nobody acknowledges. The KFC boy comes inside taking off his green hoody. Len digs his knuckles into the edge of the table, pain shooting up his wrist. He stands up, knocking his chair into the woman behind, who glares at him. He heads for the entrance, rubber soles squeaking on the linoleum. When he gets to the doors, they swing open and the sky rushes at him, thick with rain and chemicals. It's cold. People drift towards him with their motorway faces, hunched under hoods and umbrellas, blurring into the rows of cars. He strides through, hunching his shoulders against the fat drops, face gleaming with all kinds of wet. He finds the butler's car. Its dirt-spangled headlights squint back at him. He digs the key out of his pocket and pushes it into the door.

Breathes out.

Breathes in.

Thinks for half a second about the woman, just the woman herself, apart from all the things everyone else wanted her to be. All her life she lived in that city, but now when he goes back she won't be there anymore and though it's not as though he often saw her, it was more than often that she appeared, quite real, quite personally, at the edge of his vision, and it's unnerving to think that now if she does so there'll be nothing behind her. She'll be only that: a handful of incomplete memories, impossible to corroborate or confirm.

He opens the door of the butler's Audi and climbs in, slams the door and fastens his seatbelt. The key turns with a smooth growl and Len grips the top of the steering wheel, squeezing his eyes shut once to clear them.

And it's right then, in that slick revving motion, that Len Ward has an idea.

o   o

Half past eleven and he's outside the house.

The funeral is due to begin in fifteen minutes. It's lucky he wasn't invited, because he's in no mood for conversation. Though he would've preferred not being told at all to that humiliating call from Ivan's cousin. The only regret he has is Lila. He still hasn't been able to ring her.

Only once, twenty years ago, has Len stood here before. Lila's lifetime ago and yet the facade is unchanged, curtains drawn across the windows like badly healed scars. Is it something in this inertia that holds him now, preventing him from beginning what he took three buses and walked a mile to do? It's a large house over three floors, though unlike the angular towers along the rest of the street, the loft hasn't been converted. It's a family house. The kind of house bought by young couples planning babies in times such things were still possible. Len has never lived in a house like this, though he's worked on many. In this way he understands their physiology. He has a fondness for bricks and mortar, windows, tiles and roofs that he can't explain, though he tried once, to his daughter, attempting to make her see that what's most interesting isn't always what people believe will be. For instance, now it's the bins that Len notices, how they're shoved to one side as though the owner of the house considers himself too busy, too serious to replace them after the collection.

He notices also how the brick wall has been painted white in one thick coat that splashes onto the pavement at the front and the tiled path behind. The front of the house is pebble-dashed, an ugly postwar cost-saving fashion that throughout his career Len has advised his clients to replace. There's a chewing gum wrapper resting on the doormat and the letterbox is jammed open. A sticker reading NO JUNK MAIL is aslant under a stained-glass window. The tiled path, however, has been weeded. This makes Len smile with half his mouth. The other half holds a cigarette. It's this cigarette — the plastic, stale taste signalling its end — that prompts Len to action. He tosses the butt and pushes open the gate. In his pocket is a stiff coil of wire, a flat-headed screwdriver and a penknife, plus a tab of wire wool, just in case. Though if the lock is as he remembers, it won't come to that. Although forgetful in the practical sense, disorganised, reliably late, Len's memory for details is not. So it doesn't surprise him to see that the lock at the centre of the brown-painted door is indeed a 60mm Yale 89.

He works standing up so as not to attract attention — a casual visitor waiting on an answer to the bell — one hand threading the wire into the slot and the other working in the tip of the screwdriver. His fingers press and shift, flick the screwdriver and withdraw it gently, push it again, a little higher this time. He clears his throat, continuing with his visitor act, imagining he's there to deliver a parcel, perhaps a leaflet about God, though of course the obvious reason is that he's here for the funeral, hence the suit.

But soon he can't help it, he's thinking about who else has stood here and how many times — how many days and nights and mornings, afternoons, wrong times and right times, hungry times and angry times, rushed times and bored times, lazy times and anxious times, Violet pushed her true copy of the key into the door and agreed to be home.

Twenty years of guessing and Len still doesn't know why. There are obvious choices — money, property, freedom — but he can never fit them with Violet. Others he can't fit with Ivan. At times he's made up stories — outlandish pyramid schemes, a conspiracy with human puppets, the wrong brand of shaving foam — and believed them for months, sometimes years. But Len's overwhelming certainty as he slides and pokes the wire, presses his body weight against the door, is that what she did it for was all this guessing. What his most frank friend said to him once: "To me, mate, she stinks of a failed actress."

All at once the force of this impression is shattered as the wire slips and Len is thrown forward. His breath catches in his throat as he overbalances, and then shock gives way to amazement as the door opens and the hallway blinks behind it.

He doesn't have long. It's 11:48 already. Funerals are regularly as short as forty-five minutes — his dad's was a mean fifteen. He tells himself to concentrate. Never before in his life has Len so feared his own distraction.

The carpet is a beige that matches the door and on the wall is a brightly coloured print of a rural landscape. The lights are off and the quiet feels fragile, but the air is thick with something. A thick smell. Death? Or something worse? He tiptoes to the back of the house. If he got the time wrong. If he heard it wrong, mixed it up on the bad line. He has to get to the shed — Violet's 'summerhouse'. He knew from Lila it was where Violet slept. Eccentric, yes, Violet always was, but an employee of an international market research firm — what was she doing out there? Excuses ran thin. Made your bed, didn't you Violet.

The back door is adjacent to the living room door. He tells himself not to get distracted but all the same as his fingers touch the thin hoop of the mortice key, his eyes slip to the right.

Oh Jesus.

It's nothing like the miserable wallpapered room he knew from pictures Lila had shown him, with its sad worn-out sofa and the framed photo of Lila on the mantelpiece they didn't deserve. It's not a living room at all today, but a jungle, a tropical greenhouse. All he can see is flowers.

Flowers. Flowers heaped upon flowers, beneath flowers, beside flowers. The room is stuffed with them. He goes in to investigate and sneezes. His eyes sting. His skin starts to fizz like his flesh is frothing up. He sneezes, coughs, sneezes again. Every surface is covered in flowers. And cards. Rows and rows of cards dangling from strings hooked over picture hooks, shelves, doors. Like Christmas. But it isn't Christmas. Len pulls the nearest card off the string. On the front is a watercolour lily. Inside is printed 'SORRY FOR YOUR LOSS' and underneath, a biro scrawl: "We are here for you Ivan, constantly, at this terrible, terrible time". Something clamps in Len's chest. He coughs, willing his hand to tuck the card back in line while another part of him orders himself to tear it to pieces, crush it to a ball, tear them all down and burn them, kick the vases to the floor and set the room alight, the heads of carnations, lilies, white roses crackling into the carpet. Take a sledgehammer to the walls, explode the TV, run screaming into the street with that photo of Lila, carry it off in his van — damn the dead van! there is no damn van, he can't get used to it — but that photograph — whose is it now? God knows it shouldn't be Ivan's. He could torture the room until it agrees to undo everything, spit his wife out, let his life go. Because it isn't right that she sat on those grey cushions, watched the news on that TV, rested her feet on that low table, slid books onto those shelves, drew those curtains, felt the sun from that window, while he was forced to do the same without her, give their daughter only ever a home without her, that now she's died and he's in this house being ridiculed by flowers and cards for how long he's been without her.

He begins to cry and the tears are useful because they clear the pollen from his eyes and he can see again and then he can walk again and then he can't tell one flower from another, one card from another, the handwriting of people he believed were his friends from the handwriting of those who betrayed him from the start, from the alien scripts he'll never know. He drops the crumpled card he's holding and it flops open on the carpet. He finds the back door again, gasping.

Your loss.

Those cards should be addressed to Violet.

He turns the key, shoves the door, steps outside and can breathe again, shuts the door behind him. OK. One blink and there's the shed.

For one second he sees it clearly at the end of the garden before images of his wife and her husband spill across the grass. Violet planting daffodils, Violet hanging washing, Ivan smiling to himself as he comes out to help her, Ivan shirtless, Violet shoeless, both of them on sun loungers on the patio. Violet's bare feet. Toes like a hobbit, she had. Proud of them too. She was beautiful yes, Len thought so anyway, but not vain at all, though people were surprised by that, often mistook her for glamourous. She used to say her wrinkles were what tied her to the future. Used to tease him when he got a haircut, said he was strutting. Was Ivan glamorous? He always wore a shirt and cologne. Hands that touched only money and computer keyboards his whole life.

Bought her expensive dresses, Lila said, and Violet never wore them, gave them to charity. Len could've bought her expensive dresses if he'd known all she wanted was someone who bought her things she didn't want.

What's she being buried in? The question freezes him. He's surprised to note a feeling of protectiveness. It's not something he's felt towards Violet in a long time. But dead, couldn't Ivan do her up any way he wanted? Might've dressed her in silk, slipped on a bracelet of his own nail clippings. His own refrigerated doll. For a moment, Len has the conviction that Ivan is a necrophiliac, that he wanted Violet only for this reason, knew somehow she would die first, die young while he still had his virility, perhaps he even killed her, not killed her but jostled her towards death, hungry for his chance. A hotness rises in Len and he's surprised again when his protectiveness hardens into rivalry. He can't remember then what the bad thing could be, what might be so wrong with necrophilia, if it's still her body, the same body he's imagined the textures and planes and contours of for so long. He wants her, really wants her then. He's breathless thinking it, buzz in his limbs telling him to run and find her, tear her from the coffin, tear off her expensive dress and press his warm body against her.

The dead belong to nobody, Nelly said.

Bad thoughts. Len shakes his head. Wrong thoughts. Sick, he must be. He stares at the dandelions. They stare back, repulsed.

Violet loved dandelions. Determined little bastards, she called them. Focus on the dandelions. The garden is full of them. But they start to loom larger, to taunt him. He never imagined he could be jealous of dandelions, their gloating, fat buttery faces. He looks up, sees a lime tree. Jealous of a tree. He stares at the path. It shouldn't be possible to feel jealous of concrete slabs. They're wonky, need relaying, but he wants to kick them, kiss them, lick the cells that might be stored there. Her cells but who else's? It's like a house grown through with knotweed. Some of his toughest jobs: working with, working against knotweed — it rots a house. But if you love the walls, the structure, you'll do anything not to knock it down. You'll want to kiss it, kick it, kill it, because didn't it let the knotweed in?

A wood pigeon eyes him from next-door's tyre swing.

Len sprints the last paces to the shed and takes the handle. Cold metal. It's the cold that makes him afraid.

Ten past twelve. Fuck, he's late. He turns the handle but the door won't budge. It's locked.

Of course it's locked. Fucking idiot. What did you expect? It's a mortice, break your arm picking it. No sign of a key. Where's he going to find the key? A sickening deadness creeps into him. He was counting on half an hour once he was in there. It's tiny, a tiny thing. Needs time to look around. Stupid old fuck. He bangs his head against the door.

"There's one thing you should take back."

That's what she said. Like she was talking about an old shirt, though he knew what she meant immediately. She knew he would. He said, "And how would I do that?" and she said, "You've always had your ways." The tenderness between them. Unbearable. But when he couldn't speak to respond, she must've mistaken his silence for bitterness because in a sharper voice she added, "It's in the box."

He hadn't asked which box. He thought he knew which box. There was only one box — or there had been. He cursed himself for being such a gormless romantic. Ivan would've asked. Ivan would've made certain. Ivan would've found out who it was she was whispering to late at night.

He pictures the almond-shaped ruby, the smooth silver, and a rush of sensation arrives with it — the texture of her fingertips, scar at her wrist, how it caught on the bone when he tried to slide it on. Her wedding ring. Same as her engagement. It had been his grandmother's, and he couldn't afford another. She didn't want another, she said. But when Ivan proposed he gave her a diamond, Lila said, and after they got married he pressed a gold wedding band over it. Deposit, down payment, remittance. Now if Len doesn't find it, his grandmother's ring will also be Ivan's. He has to get it. He tries the handle twice more in an insincere procrastination, then turns and jogs back up the path.

It's insane that he counted on it being left open. Violet was a woman who locked the kitchen door when she made tea. Violet is, he corrects himself. *The dead don't change.* Ivan will probably be reincarnated as a dead bolt. Well. Heart racing, he reaches the back door, opens it and steps inside, breathing through his mouth to avoid the smell. He scans above and below the door for the key, no luck. Under the door. Attached to the other key? No.

In the living room, he steps over and around flowers, runs his hands along the shelves, windowsill: nothing. Checks the drawers: nothing. Spots a hoop of something metal on the mantelpiece and rushes over, almost tripping on a potted orchid, and it's not a key at all but a smooth gold ring. Violet's wedding ring. The other one. The wrong one. Len gasps, jumps, drops it and it glints from the carpet, cursing him. A single righteous handcuff. He steps backwards, knocking into the orchid, scattering clumps of soil over the carpet. He stoops to pile it back into the pot before knocking a vase onto his shoe, soaking his socks and the carpet.

You're panicking, Len.

He stands up. Breathes. Shakes his foot, rights the vase, the orchid, stares at the dark patch on the carpet and looks around for something to press on it. Finding nothing, he checks the time again and almost chokes to see how late it's got, gives up and jogs to the kitchen. It'll dry. It's hot in there. It'll easily dry.

In the kitchen, three or four dozen bottles of wine line the table, two long trays covered in tinfoil, a crate of Becks beside the fridge, another of orange juice. There's a handwritten note stuck to the fridge with, Len realises, his own telephone number written on it. He remembers Ivan's cousin's voice on the phone. Same sharp monotone as Ivan. "Keys," Len says aloud, shouting over the memory of that voice. "Keys, keys, keys." There's a corkboard between two cupboards with a photograph of Violet in a chair and Ivan standing behind her, hands gripping her shoulders. The windowsill looks onto the street. Any minute now. And no key.

Len weighs up the alternatives: check upstairs, or break one of the shed windows and climb in.

It's not likely the key is upstairs, but there's a small chance the ring will be — didn't women keep things like that in their bedrooms? If it's up there, he'll have smashed a window for nothing. But he's sure she meant the shed. And if he's caught ransacking their bedroom there'll be far more serious, possibly legal, trouble. On top of this he has no desire to see their bed.

He decides to take five minutes to attempt the lock with the equipment he has, since perhaps it's old and less sturdy than he imagines, and if not he'll smash one of the side windows. That way it might not be noticed until tomorrow.

He wipes his forehead on his sleeve and rushes back along the hall. With his hand on the back door, he cringes. Is he really going to smash the window of his dead ex-wife's shed? It seems... extreme. He checks the time. 12:22. Fuck, fuck, fuck.

He looks around, almost hoping they'll turn up right then, get it over with. But when he looks around he sees a door. A door he hadn't noticed before. A cupboard door. The cupboard under the stairs. He walks up to it. There's a latch. It opens with a small click. Damp smell. Dark under there. There's a rack of wine along the back wall, a hoover, two large suitcases, a heap of coats grown together with mould. The gas meter.

No key.

Len closes the door.

Closes the door with a jangle.

There was a jangle. He opens it again: another jangle. There, on the back of the door: three keys hung on three separate nails, neatly labeled Front, Back and Shed. Thank you God for organised bastards. Len plucks the Shed key and shuts the door. Once outside he locks the back door and pockets that key too, before jogging back up the path.

The Shed key slides into the lock. It turns. He removes the key and opens the door. Once he's inside, he pulls the door shut and locks it behind him.

Violet.

In a moment he'll be able to see again. Until then it's only the two of them — her and him and then, back then, once again the two of them and the summer and their flat, the living room, smell of two faces loving against the carpet.

o   o   o

Time to get to work. When Len's eyes have adjusted, he takes account of his surroundings, scanning for a place to begin. The shed is finished in the classic style. Nordic, stained plywood, a simple electrical set-up. There's a desk, a bed, two shelves, dirty-looking curtains, a ragrug by the door and a blanket on the bed.

He recognises that blanket. Used to be his, that did. He steps forward, rubs it between two fingers. Hadn't even known it was gone.

What did she do out here?

Only these walls as witnesses.

What he would give to have been a witness.

Is that what love is? Just to keep on wanting and wanting to be a witness?

He sits down on the bed, pulling the blanket out from under him, folding it on his knee.

He should get up, he knows that. He knows what this sitting down means, this folding of the blanket. He should get up. He will do. Just a minute. Just one minute to take it all in — what was she doing here? — one minute to think this blanket through. No he doesn't want to look yet — not to look and find, nor to look and not find, and either way give up this moment to the past. No he wants a minute more, just one minute more to soak her up. Nobody watching. He leans back, leans until he can feel the covers on his cheek and then he's there, anyway, so he might as well lie down. He stretches out, pulling the blanket up to his chin. One minute, that's all. But Jesus Christ, how is it possible for a person to carry around the same smell for so many years? It's a wonder it doesn't age like the skin. After all, scents are famous for going stale — take the lily. That living room will reek before the week is out.

Violet's body will have lost her scent by now. That's what shocked him the most with his dad — how the body smelt of nothing at all. He thought it must be a fake, a wax work, a switch to save his feelings. He was eighteen. He would have liked to smell his dad one last time. His mum he didn't know long enough to recall her smell, though you'd think the brain would store that information somewhere. It occurs to him that he gave his daughter much the same life as his own, though the new generation replaced death with desertion. A smash for a slap. He did try to mother Lila but frankly, he's never been sure what a mother does exactly.

Bad memory: Lila anxiety-racked, thumb-sucking,

stoned, skipping her GCSEs out of a paralysis she called *I'm fucked, like just totally fucked*, Violet's retort: "What is she? a complete imbecile?" Yes, mother, our daughter struggled five times as much as the other kids just to learn how to spell, add, speak, write.

He sinks back, turns around and buries his face in the pillow. If she's anywhere now it must be here where the grease and cells of her continue to mix with air and cotton, where her DNA remains in sweat, possibly urine, it's not clear how far things went. Bowel cancer — Len's heart churns. She must've been so afraid.

He opens his eyes, remembering something Lila told him. About a time she came here to visit. She said after they'd been talking for an hour or so Violet stopped Lila mid-sentence, grabbed her wrist and said she had a mission. Violet was always giving Lila missions. Anyway she told Lila to go to the desk and look in the second drawer down on the left and — Len can still picture Lila's impression, wide eyes, dancing fingers — "See what you can find."

Len sits up. The drawer has a keyhole but isn't locked. He shuffles forward on the bed, leans forward and opens it. It's heavy. It sticks and judders. Inside is a wad of paper. He stands up, lifts this out, scratching the back of his hand on the tip of a screw, places the paper on the table. Then he laughs.

The red cap sticks out from a wrap of black fabric. He unwraps it. Glen's, of course. So Nelly was right. People don't change. Pretty tinkling swish. He unscrews the lid and sniffs it.

Recoils.

Sniffs again.

Imagines his daughter handing it to her mother. The cold and the weight of the bottle, the pride and the pain of the action. Just a month or so ago. That's all he wanted to know, isn't it? He puts the bottle down. It's all he wanted to know. He's not going to drink any. Of course he's not.

He won't. Just needed to know. For himself. If Lila was telling the truth. Not exaggerating. If Violet was still — Lila did sometimes exaggerate — he just wanted to check.

He himself doesn't drink. Hasn't drunk in thirteen years.

He stares at the vodka. Tips it back and forth. Unscrews the lid to sniff it again, replaces the lid. Scraping twist of it.

Something in the glug of the liquid in the heavy bottle, the tinkling crystal sound of it, its clarity, makes him think of bells and fairies, rushing water, magical places, the stuff of childhood, more Lila's than his, and the sadness of it all: the bottle in the drawer, the dying flowers, this old man, old cuckold, smelling the sheets in his dead ex-wife's bed. It's intoxicating, a potent mix. It's difficult to believe he isn't drunk already.

Ah, life.

It's over before you know it, anyway.

Get drunk on champagne and vodka — she's your new life.

He pictures Lila's face and her eyes are like slaps.

But what difference will it make?

No one out here. No one looking for him. No place to be. No job in the morning.

One drink and then he'll ring Lila. He'll be able to ring her, then. He'll ring her and explain — catch her on her way between the funeral and the wake. Perhaps they can arrange to meet after. That's exactly what he should do. It's what he should've done all along.

He needs something to get him through until after.

It probably won't affect him. One sip. Just a sip for the road.

He's saving Ivan the shame of finding it. A generous act.

He shuts his eyes. Tries one last time. Then grits his teeth and unscrews the cap.

When he's given up telling himself he's going to put it straight back, Len takes the bottle and lies down on the bed. Takes another gulp because it makes his mouth feel calm.

The ceiling is tracked with woodworm. They'll need treating soon with Permathrin or it'll start raining dust. He could've sorted that for Violet. He could've built her a shed that wouldn't rot. He has another gulp for that, and another for the woodworm, and then he tosses the bottle to the edge of the bed.

Lovely warm feeling coming up from his belly.

He could've made her even warmer than that.

He shakes his head. He needs to get up, needs to check the time. It could be any time by now, it could be too late. He should check it. Instead he rolls onto his side and reaches down to retrieve the bottle, takes another swig.

Holy vodka. A monk in his cell. He rolls back onto his back, stretches his arms up. Violet often said she wanted to be a monk. No, the word she used was *hermit*. She said hermit and he teased her she wanted to be a crab. He should've taken her dreams more seriously. On one of his days off, one of three he took in three months there in the New Forest, Len drove down to Dorset for the day. He set off at four a.m. to arrive by six thirty and miss the crowds, dawn putting psychedelic patterns in the shingle. He watched the seafoam crash and disappear before the bulge of the water, so the submerged pebbles stretched and swelled underneath. It was a thick film over everything, the sea, and it could be peeled off in one piece. That's what it looked like — like peeling gorilla tape off a wall, and it would drag all its filaments, its creatures and secrets up with it. But not the crab. The crab would be safe. It just went. The tide went out, the wave rolled away and the crab sank into shingle — a stain fading under multiple coats of paint in that tricksy way where you have to blink and change the light or you can still see it.

Crab-watching his whole life.

After, he walked six miles to Burton Bradstock and ate fish and chips off his knees looking out over the Channel towards France and chatted to the man who owned the boat rental until it was too dark to walk back so he took the bus and the Green Goddess was at the corner where he'd left her and he drove back listening to Dylan's 'Duquesne Whistle' on repeat because Lila had sent him the new album. Probably the best day this year, that was.

He heaves himself up to sit on the edge of the bed and finds himself face to face with Ivan. Something lurches inside him. He grips his knees. It's only a photo. But even behind glass Ivan looks pleased with himself. Len takes the picture off the wall and puts it face down on the desk. There's a dark rectangle where it was hung. Very dark. All that bleaching, all that time. Len rubs his hands over his face and hair, stands up. The vodka's made him heavy. He leans on the desk to steady himself and then his nose is right up against the shelves.

Right up against a box on the shelves.

Not a box. The box.

It's the box. Right there, in among all those books, fat art books on one side and paperbacks on the other. It's a wonder he didn't see it straight away. But all those fucking books. Jealous of every one of them, her cells snug in the pages. He's about to reach for the box but stops short, takes the bottle and screws the lid on as tightly as he can, places it back in the drawer and shuts the drawer, hard.

Thank God for that. He's going to be fine now.

A minute later he opens the drawer again, takes out the bottle and downs the last inch. Then he puts it back, shoves the papers in on top and knees the drawer shut, cursing himself.

His throat burns. His heart burns. His eyes burn.

The world is burning.

Or is it Violet burning that very moment and he's still got that old matrimonial sixth sense?

His head sways. He squints, crinkling and stretching his face to clear it. Then finally he reaches for the box.

It's stuck. Stickiness of wood on wood, he has to move a book on shamanism to get it out. Both leave dark brown rectangles on the shelf. He puts the book back and places the box on the desk, running his fingertips under the lip.

He can smell booze, smell it on himself.

He cuffs his mouth. Looks around.

For a moment, he considers giving up. Just walking out and going home right then. Not looking in the box, not finding anything, just walking out. Maybe calling Lila. Finding a cafe nearby where he could wait to meet her. Pretending none of this ever happened. But then a branch snaps outside and the noise makes him jump and before he can think anything else about it, his fingers have flipped the lid.

For several seconds, Len can't see or hear anything, it is like his head will explode. Then his heart slows and he can see again and the inside of the box stares back.

He blinks. He tilts the box. He turns it towards the light.

As though light could make black velvet turn into silver and ruby. He presses his fingers inside it, into every corner. He turns it upside down and shakes it. He bangs it on the desk. He looks inside it again. Then all at once he is exhausted. He reaches backwards, wanting to sit down. He reaches, aiming for the bed but misses it, sliding to the floor with a jerk in the back of his leg that makes him yelp and his head smack forward against the desk leg.

Deserved that.

He tastes the blood streaming from his tongue and tries to figure out what world he thought he was living in.

There is no ring. The box is empty. Violet is dead. He's a drunk old fantasist burgling the house of a grief-ridden stranger.

For what feels like hours, Len crouches there, sucking the blood from his tongue and figuring between histories. It's not clear what has happened and what hasn't. If there ever was a ring, a phone call, a daughter, three months in the middle of nowhere, a wife.

If there ever was a life.

He shuts his eyes, running back over images, while his back starts to ache and his legs cramp. He hauls himself back onto the bed. Face in his hands. Jesus Christ. Smell of him. Smell of this old man. He can't even smell Violet in the smell of this old man. He spreads his fingers, looking out to see what's left. If there's anything left of her, if he hasn't broken it all up. If he didn't make it all up. He sees the frame face down on the desk and starts to shrink with shame. He leans forward to pick it up, set it straight. But then he notices something tucked into the back, under the wire. Another photo. He takes it out.

Lila.

That face. He couldn't have dreamt up that face. Lila's little face. And it's doing its trick for him, see? Going Violet, Len, Violet, Len, Violet, as he squints at it. Six or seven years old, she must be. Raggedy hair clashing with a yellow t-shirt so big it hangs almost to her knees. Standing outside where? Looks like the park by Len's old place.

Their daughter. They had a daughter. They had a child and so it is definitely true that they had sex at least once. At least! Christ, Len, give yourself some credit. They had sex hundreds of times, thousands — who was counting? Or who was counting back then?

The daughter is certain. And so why not the wife,

the life, the ring, the bed they shared and her skin, stomach, breasts, legs? Christ, don't, Christ, her tongue. Jesus fuck. Don't, but — then where does the not stop?

She chucked it, that's what happened. Hurt Ivan's feelings so she chucked it. Jealousy always got its own way.

He checks the box again.

It's just a ring. Was just.

He sits down holding the box. He lies back and lifts it to his face. It smells musty, leathery. She always had this box. He was never allowed to look in it. That was why they both knew he knew what she meant when she said *in the box*. There was only one box. He's waited his whole life to look in this damn box.

Maybe the box was the one thing. Maybe this is what she meant. They hadn't understood each other twenty years ago, why would they any better after that long apart?

He twirls it over his eyes, remembering the place it used to be, once upon a time, at the back of her desk, same desk, in the corner of their living room. He always wanted to live with a woman who had a desk, was fascinated by desks, never himself being able to sit at one for any length of time. Lila inherited this predicament from him — *imbecile* — could still hear her saying it — feel the gut-punch of knowing he'd given his daughter a mother who referred to her own child as an *imbecile* — and she inherited from her mother that voice, that same voice that said imbecile — though not the character to say it — but the same voice Len also remembers whispering better things like *I love you, I want you, come here, fuck me, do you want spaghetti again for dinner? we'll buy her a real yellow teddy bear when she comes.*

He hates her. Hated her. That she could do all that.

And yet there he is, lying on her bed, clamped inside this endless want.

It doesn't matter how dead she is, nothing changes she's still what he wants.

He's been so far away from everything.

"Violet?" he says.

The room says nothing.

He starts chuckling. "You poor deluded bastard."

He drops the box behind his head and stares at the ceiling. He remembers he's wearing a suit and that in fact, he looked quite sharp when he left home. It's true he's handsome, also true that he's a good dad, most of the time, and talented, despite his best efforts at self-sabotage. He's not old — 58! He's healthy, has decades ahead of him. Maybe even another wife. He could date someone Violet's age — old age, as in previous age, as in 33, her age when they met — if he was that way inclined. It's the way of the world these days, as a man, you just copy and paste yourself back where you want to be, it's the women who lose out.

The trouble was, he didn't want anybody else.

He sits up, stretching his arms behind him. Not much left of him that can listen to all this. He finds his own ring and tugs it. Twists it up and down the first section of knuckle. It hurts. He'll need a hacksaw to get it off.

Hacksaw — that's exactly what he needs. Not another ring, but to get rid of this one. He has to get it off. He tugs it, wincing with the dagger-pain that bursts through the knuckle, shoves it in his mouth for lubrication then tugs it with his teeth — like being smacked in the molars. He needs tools. Needs just one minute with a hacksaw and some antiseptic ready if he slips.

Enough. This has all been a mistake. He lurches up, reaches the door and turns the key, turns the handle, pushes it wide to meet the icy glaze of autumn.

It's only five past two. He might just get away with it.

o   o   o   o

Halfway across the garden, Len realises he won't get away with anything. Past the window of the living room and the frosted glass of the back door, bodies glide like storm clouds. No one looks out. He could stand here all afternoon, probably, and nobody would look out. If he chucked a rock through the window, probably nobody would look out. An indignation sets in, and he opens his mouth to say something, but finds that the only word he's got is *Violet*.

VIOLET.

What if he ran in shouting it? What if she ran out?

But she's not there anymore. She's not anywhere. He has to keep reminding himself of that. What all these people mean at this moment, Len realises, is that her body no longer exists. They burned her. These people stood swapping sadness and pity while her body was legally, ritually burned. Then some official would've given Ivan a box. In the box would be her ashes. He could run his hands through her, if he wanted. Ivan could. He could scoop her into cups. Maybe Len could have a cupful. Ashes could be shared out so much more easily than a person. They could do it proportionally, by the years. Ivan wouldn't miss one little bit. One matchbox. One spoonful.

An urgency rushes up through Len, pressing at his throat and he jogs the last few metres to the back door, grabs the handle and remembers it's locked. He fumbles for the key, shoves it in and grabs again, his eyes catching on his ring — the hacksaw! the plan! the daughter! whole shitting mess of his life.

Ah, fuck.

He opens the door.

A tall, bony man with glasses walks past, smelling a glass of wine. Behind him people are crammed together, some talking, some trying to get through. Nobody looks at Len. There's a smell of toasted cheese masking the flowers. Who are these people? Good idea to have the wake in such a small space — makes it feel like the dead person had friends. Loved ones.

Loved ones — what kind of term is that? What about the unloved ones? What about the ones who loved?

All these strangers saw her coffin. They sang and prayed and saw her coffin roll off. While Len — don't.

He licks his lips. Yes, his lips have something. Lips have something nobody else in this room will ever have. Violet's vodka. Her bottle. Her lips on the bottle and then his. Her lips.

He steps into the hall and tugs the door shut behind him. A woman wearing for some reason a bright purple hat stuck with feathers nods at him and moves on into the living room. Len follows, fixing his gaze on the carpet to avoid the flowers. But when a broad woman pushes past, he looks up to watch where he's going and jolts in confusion.

The putrid greenhouse he remembers, swarming with green and fetid grey and that rich, creeping smell is gone. There are bunches, yes, but not dozens. A dozen, maybe, lined up on the table and along the mantelpiece. One large bunch in a vase in front of the TV. A single string of cards hangs over the sofa. He stares at a particularly wilted bunch of lilies, before a sharpness in his forehead threatens sobriety. He makes his way to the wine table.

Maybe they moved them upstairs to make room for the mourners. An image of all those bouquets decking out Ivan's bedroom, the sad man weeping at the centre, braces Len and he scolds himself, leans against the wall, looks at his shoes. He needs to concentrate.

What Violet was and what she wasn't. Death. Mud. Vodka. This moth-bitten old suit. Moth-bitten old man. Strangers in a house that will always be strange to him.

Finally, the person in front finishes his immense task of opening a new bottle and pouring himself a single glass. Len nabs the bottle and an abandoned glass and glugs the red liquid full to the brim. Then because a few people are waving empty glasses close by, he pours a drink each for them too. He's being helpful. He doesn't have to be helpful. He could take the bottle. He could drink the whole bottle. He could take the bottle and lob it at the ceiling. He could take the bottle, lob it at the wall, hard enough to smash it to pieces. He could take a shard and cut off his ring finger. Douse it in alcohol and stick it in a frame above the telly as proof he'd once had a life.

He downs the glass, drums the ring on the table, pours another. A grey-haired lady and a short round man with a halo of tight curls eye him expectantly until he realises he's still holding the bottle and fills their glasses, puts it down. They thank him and walk off. All these strangers. He thought there'd be someone here he knew. Maybe Ivan banished them too. There must be more people in the kitchen. Ivan must be in the kitchen.

He sips his wine. Should not be drinking — the thought eyes him from the deep of his belly — well — there are worse things. He hasn't killed anyone. Hasn't ruined anybody's life.

"DAD."

Her voice cuts through the room and Len ducks his head towards the wall. Wants to see her, yes, but did she have to give the game away? She comes over and tries to hug him but he hustles her into the corner.

"Dad," she says. "What are you doing here? Were you at the church? I thought you weren't coming. Dad, why are you looking at me like that?"

"Huh?"

"Are you drinking?" She takes him in — hair, mouth, suit, glass. "You're drinking."

"God Lila, I missed you."

"Dad?"

It's bad.

He can hear in his voice it's bad.

"Dad, come outside."

She takes the glass off him and puts it on the table, glances around and back at him. She's wearing black jeans and a black t-shirt and her hair is tied up in a black furry-looking piece of fabric. She has Violet's face and Violet's eyes and Violet's hands gripping his side and it hurts him in the ribs just to look at her.

"Baby girl," he says.

"You idiot."

"I'm sorry."

Her gaze flies over his shoulder and he feels her tense up. He doesn't need to turn around to know who she's looking at.

"Is that Len Ward?"

Len is about to say something when he sees on his daughter's face real fear. He shushes her, a reflex reaction that makes no sense and turns her fear, for just a moment, to confusion.

"I thought you said you couldn't come."

Len tries to step past Lila so she's not in between them but she won't move. She turns sideways, as though she might need to hold them apart. Her eyes dart back and forth between them, and it hits Len that it might not be Ivan she's afraid of. But it's too late to worry about that. He looks past her to get a proper look at his enemy.

Black suit, combed hair, tired-out face, grief-thin shoulders — Ivan stares at Len like he's trying to but can't quite figure something out. He puts a hand to his mouth.

Mouth that kissed Violet's mouth.

"You said you'd go some other time to the cemetery."

A powdery-looking woman appears beside Ivan, asks if everything's all right.

Ivan shakes his head. The woman looks where he's looking, right at Len. "Len Ward?" she says. "I see. We spoke on the phone, if you remember?"

Ivan's cousin. Len nods, though he's struggling to fit this person with that voice. More people turn to stare at them. Lila's hand tightens around his wrist and he looks at her. She's wincing, her face all twisted up. He opens his mouth to explain, but a memory freezes him.

Violet's knee. A dimple on it. Same one right there on Lila's chin. That dimple. A close-up version. Violet's knee. Against his face. His arms wrapped around her knees, throat rasping. This same carpet, same room, same house. Things he doesn't want to remember, doesn't want to know. Never wanted to. But that dimple, story all pouring out of it, pouring out of his daughter's face. He wants to push it away, tell her to stop it.

"Why didn't you say," Ivan is saying, "if you'd changed your mind?"

Len feels the ground move underneath him. He moves closer to Lila, tries to find her hand with his. "I just wanted one thing," he says.

"One thing?" Ivan says.

The powdery-cousin's face fills the room.

"Yeah. But what would you know about anything?"

Len says.

"Dad?" Lila says. "Let's go."

The two men stare at each other, and Len is fixed by the stare, as though if he moved his skin would come off. Then a deadness sets in, and a cold realisation with it.

None of this means anything.

Not the funeral, the wife, the life, the ring. None of it matters one bit. Everything in the universe is closer now than Violet. The sun will explode and she'll still be dead.

"Is he drunk?" the cousin says.

"He's fine," Lila says.

Ivan takes his eyes off Len and looks at Lila. "I thought he didn't drink," he says.

"He's obviously drunk." The cousin again.

Lila says, "I'll take him home."

"If you want to be so generous," Ivan says.

"I'll ring him a taxi." The cousin.

"I said I'll take him."

Len tries to shake his head but realises it's not moving. He watches his daughter suck her cheeks and flare her eyes and knows she's trying not to cry.

"I'll ring you both a taxi," the cousin says. "But take him outside. He needs fresh air. This isn't the place for him.

There are grieving guests."

"That's right," Len says. "Nothing but guests to grief, all of them." He starts to laugh and Lila pulls him towards her. The cousin mutters something under her breath. Ivan thumbs his eyes.

"We'll take the bus," Lila says.

"Whatever you like."

"Come on Dad," she says.

She turns to face him. She looks older at that moment than he's ever seen her. At the same time he smells her smell. Forgotten daughter smell. She pulls his hand to her face and kisses it and Len realises far too late that it's not her but him who's going to cry.

"I didn't say I couldn't come," he rasps. "They told me not to. They said. Lila, they told me not to. Think I would miss it? Think I would've missed it for any stupid little thing?"

She is shaking her head, not breaking eye contact. "No," she says. "No, Dad, course not." Then because he can't hold it any longer and it's as though the room is already busting with the force of the fight he's putting up against it, he pulls his arms up to his chest, tries to shout but instead comes out with a gurgling, ripping animal sound that surprises everyone including himself, and pulls away from Lila, pushing past Ivan and the cousin towards the door. He takes one last look around. A crowd has formed. They're staring at him. Well the entertainment is over now, they can go back to being heartbroken. He gathers himself, shouldering through the bodies crammed in the corridor. For people who want him to leave, they're doing a good job of trapping him here.

Who are you? Len wants to shout at them. What do any of you have to do with Violet? She was my whole life.

"Come on, mate, out."

Two men have followed Len to the door, taking on bouncer duty. One opens the front door and the other steers Len by the shoulders.

"What do you mean 'mate'?" Len says, shrugging him off.

They exchange glances behind his back. The man on Len's right smells of mothballs. The other smells of something high-pitched, mosquito-like. They both have bony, academic's arms — if Len wasn't so dilapidated by booze he could take them out easily. Not that he wants to take them out. What he wants is to lie down somewhere hard and flat.

They manoeuvre him through the door onto the front step. Old door, old enemy. The lock he picked so easily a few hours earlier. Friendly traitor Yale. It occurs to Len that he left his tools somewhere and he curses himself. It would've been better not to remember. Ivan's tools now. The men deliver him to the pavement and go back inside.

A moment later, Lila appears. "Dad," she says from the doorway.

He cuffs the back of his head in a kind of wave.

"I'm coming with you," she says.

"No you're not."

"I am, I'm coming."

"No you're not."

She jolts and he knows his tone startled her. That's good. That's what he intended. She shrugs and he makes a peace sign and then she sighs and leans in the doorway.

"You're an idiot for getting drunk," she says, kicking her heal on the doorstep. "And for not calling me." She kicks harder. "Two weeks, Dad." Kick, kick, kick. "I was. I don't know what I was." She stops kicking and starts to chew her thumb, tears something off it and winces. "But I don't care about any of that."

Len squeezes his own thumb, feeling her pain in his.

"Dad?" she says.

He looks at her. She folds her arms, looks up the street and then back at him. "I didn't see her, Dad. Ivan wouldn't let me see her. I mean her body."

He clenches his jaw but it's no use. He has to turn away to hide his face. Wishes she was one year old again and he could hold her tight against his chest and make her happy with two arms and a heartbeat.

"Dad?" she says.

He bats his hand. Hears her sigh.

"I love you," she says. "Anyway."

"Come and see me after," he says. But she's not there to say yes or no. The door has already clicked shut.

I love you.

What a crazy thing to say to someone, he thinks. What a crazy thing to teach a child to say. Three words passed up and down generations like an automatic bonus. But it wasn't automatic. That was the mistake he'd made, perhaps.

He tries not to think of Lila inside there, Lila among all those strangers. Lila trying to find her own one thing. He tries to hold onto the good things she said and not the ones that hurt. Those will come for him later. He needs to get home. She needs him to get home. The best thing he can do for her now is get home. He spins on his heel, gripping the wall to steady himself, and forces himself to look up. The sky is enormous. Absurdly, it's still the bright middle of the afternoon. This makes him laugh. It's cold, he knows, though he can't feel it. He swings his arms to loosen his suit jacket, realising he badly needs a piss. Checking up and down the street first, he turns and leans an arm against the wall and with the other, unzips his fly. It's a relief, and the piss splashes out, and it doesn't matter that it splashes over his shoes. He pisses on Ivan's wall, smiling, shakes and fixes his fly. Then he stumbles only slightly before steadying himself, ordering his feet to keep going up the road.

Not far to his gorgeous Green Goddess — thank God he didn't give into paranoia but left her just up the road. He watches his boots step stepping on the pavement. He can see her shiny green shoulders already. Step stepping. He could use a glass of water. He could use a splash of water for his face. He could use a bucket of ice water tipped over his head. He could use a chance to start this day over again. Stay home like an ordinary ex-husband, sorting through those photos he should've thrown out years ago. Lila could have them now.

Ah, life.

There she is — green paint reflecting the sunlight.

He walks towards her. He reaches into the inside pocket of his jacket for the key, leans against her familiar side while he slides it into the lock, turns it. Lovely click of the handle, lovely creak of the door. He hoists himself up. Shuts the door. Pulls down the sunshade and checks himself in the mirror.

Drunk eyes, all right. But not bad.

He sits back.

He won't drive her, of course not, not that kind of drunk. Sleep it off first. Sleep it off. Good sleeps in here, some of the finest. He winds the seat back. Leans down to loosen his boots.

Tugs the knots in the laces. They're wet. Piss, probably. Tied tight. He tugs and picks. The knot loosens. Feet ache. Then the knot gives and he arches his foot to take it out. Flexes his toes.

Other foot, other knot. So much trouble in life.

Then something slides across his back.

He stops — not freezes, but — still for a moment. What was that?

Like fingertips... spread across his back. Long time since... fingertips. On his back. Dream stuff. Couldn't be. But — fingertips. Stroking his ribs. Unmistakeable.

No — he shakes his head. Concentrates on the knot. Mistakable. But the stroking continues.

Fingertips. Has to be.

A light tap.

He swallows, lets go of his laces, sits up just slightly, so the hand won't be obliged to move.

"Aren't you going to say hello?" she says.

He shuts his eyes. Opens them again. Sits up and the hand slides around him to rest at the top of his thigh. Always used to like resting her hand there. He sits upright, turns his head to follow where her arm must be. His eyes sliding up her body, shoulders, neck.

"It's you," he says.

She frowns at him.

He can smell her hair mixing with the diesel. He wants to touch her and he wants to stay here watching, to be about to touch her, to stay in this one moment for the rest of his life. She's got on her old teasing face. He leans forward, all at once desperate to feel the warmth coming off her. So cold. He's been so cold without her. She sighs. His eyes glance to the hand that's on his leg and he jolts.

"You're wearing it," he says.

She lifts her hand and turns it once in front of his face so he can see all around the silver band of it, the tiny red almond. She makes a fist and flings it open again, like a magician might make it disappear, but it's still there.

Then she places both palms on his face. He can feel her nails at his temple and the smooth metal band on his cheek. He knows exactly how her ears would feel if he touched them.

"What did you think," she says, "I'd lost it?"

He shakes his head. Moves her palm to his mouth and kisses it. She leans across and rests her chin on his shoulder, pressing the silk of her lips on his ear. Her breath goes through him like the ground goes in a lift.

"Violet." He tries her name again.

"I missed you," she says.

Acknowledgements

Thank you Rob True for reading the first draft, fixing my construction lingo and making Len feel all right in the world.

Thank you Sanya Semakula for all your meticulous edits and big questions.

Thank you Scott Manley Hadley, Gabriella Boyd, Alice McKeever, Rebecca Lanham, Joe Rizzo Naudi, Julie Tanner, Samar Hammam and Gabriella McGrogan for reading various stages of drafts.

Thank you Sean Preston for taking the piss out of me enough that I believed the good stuff and generally making the whole Open Pen thing happen.

Thank you Beccy for living with me and all my anxieties. Thank you Dan, Em, Tina, Gabby, Ali and Vinnie for however many conversations. Thanks to everyone I've met through Open Pen for making the writing process less panic-stricken and strange.

And thank you mother and brother for making me laugh.

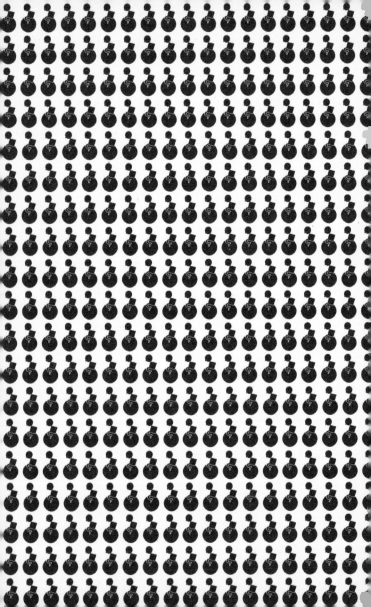